Eric
N.

MARY BETH
d Juror #23,
eme Court,
of New York,
al Narcotics
. P.

ok a Trip to the Zoo
t © 2002 by Shirley Neitzel
copyright © 2002
nslow Parker
rved.
gapore by Tien Wah Press
hildrens.com

ints, pencils, and a black
d for the full-color art.
s Seagull Light.

ress
Publication Data

trip to the zoo /
el; illustrated
w Parker.

oks."
ulative verse with rebuses
boy has a wonderful day
a series of mishaps with

-X (trade).
-8 (lib. bdg.)
uses. 2. Zoos—Fiction.
ction. 4. Stories in rhyme.]
nslow, ill. II. Title.
[E]—dc21   2001023670

4   3   2   1

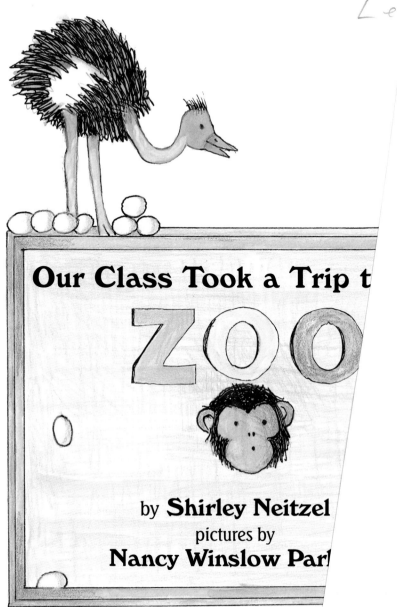

Our Class Took a Trip t

ZOO

by **Shirley Neitzel**
pictures by
Nancy Winslow Par

Greenwillow Bool

An Imprint of HarperCollinsPub

For
—S.

FOR
Gran
Supr
State
Spec
—N.

Our Class To
Text copyrig
Illustrations
by Nancy W
All rights res
Printed in Si
www.harperc

Watercolor p
pen were use
The text type

Library of Con
Cataloging-in-

Neitzel, Shirley
Our class took
by Shirley Neit
by Nancy Wins
   p.   cm.
"Greenwillow B
Summary: A cu
in which a youn
at the zoo, despi
the animals.
ISBN 0-688-1554
ISBN 0-688-1554
   1. Rebuses. [1. R
   3. Zoo animals—
   1. Parker, Nancy
PZ8.3.N34 Wd 20

   10   9 8 7 6
First Edition

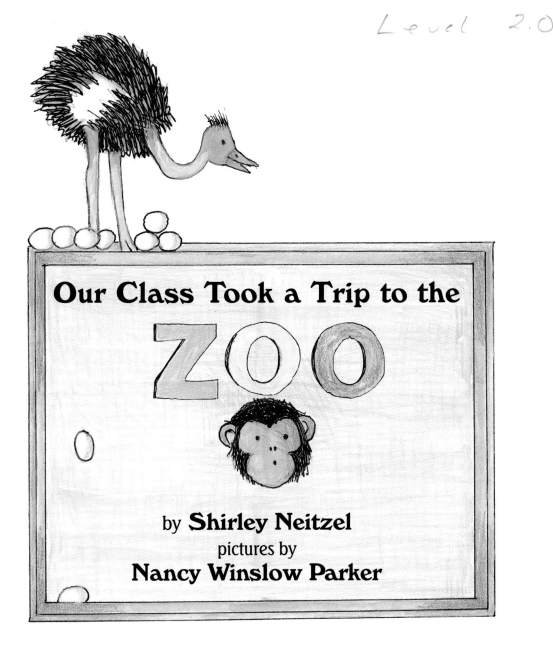

Our Class Took a Trip to the ZOO

by **Shirley Neitzel**

pictures by
Nancy Winslow Parker

Greenwillow Books
An Imprint of HarperCollins Publishers

For Eric
—S. N.

FOR MARY BETH
Grand Juror #23,
Supreme Court,
State of New York,
Special Narcotics
—N. W. P.

Our Class Took a Trip to the Zoo
Text copyright © 2002 by Shirley Neitzel
Illustrations copyright © 2002
by Nancy Winslow Parker
All rights reserved.
Printed in Singapore by Tien Wah Press
www.harperchildrens.com

Watercolor paints, pencils, and a black
pen were used for the full-color art.
The text type is Seagull Light.

Library of Congress
Cataloging-in-Publication Data

Neitzel, Shirley.
Our class took a trip to the zoo /
by Shirley Neitzel; illustrated
by Nancy Winslow Parker.
    p.   cm.
"Greenwillow Books."
Summary: A cumulative verse with rebuses
in which a young boy has a wonderful day
at the zoo, despite a series of mishaps with
the animals.
ISBN 0-688-15543-X (trade).
ISBN 0-688-15544-8 (lib. bdg.)
1. Rebuses. [1. Rebuses. 2. Zoos—Fiction.
3. Zoo animals—Fiction. 4. Stories in rhyme.]
I. Parker, Nancy Winslow, ill. II. Title.
PZ8.3.N34 Wd 2002 [E]—dc21 2001023670

10 9 8 7 6 5 4 3 2 1
First Edition

Our class took a trip to the zoo.

I left my coat with the chimpanzee

when our class took a trip to the zoo.

I dropped my lunch when the bear startled me,

and I left my with the chimpanzee

when our class took a trip to the zoo.

I tore my pants on the ostriches' pen,

I dropped my when the bear startled me,

and I left my with the chimpanzee

when our class took a trip to the zoo.

A button popped off by the lions' den,

I tore my on the ostriches' pen,

I dropped my when the bear startled me,

and I left my with the chimpanzee

when our class took a trip to the zoo.

My hat blew away

near Billy Goat Mountain,

a popped off by the lions' den,

I tore my on the ostriches' pen,

I dropped my when the bear startled me,

and I left my with the chimpanzee

when our class took a trip to the zoo.

My shirt got wet at the water fountain,

my blew away near Billy Goat Mountain,

a popped off by the lions' den,

I tore my on the ostriches' pen,

I dropped my when the bear startled me,

and I left my with the chimpanzee

when our class took a trip to the zoo.

My shoes got muddy when I fed a duck,

my got wet at the water fountain,

my blew away near Billy Goat Mountain,

a popped off by the lions' den,

I tore my on the ostriches' pen,

I dropped my when the bear startled me,

and I left my with the chimpanzee

when our class took a trip to the zoo.

My dime rolled under the ice cream truck,

my got muddy when I fed a duck,

my got wet at the water fountain,

my blew away near Billy Goat Mountain,

a popped off by the lions' den,

I tore my on the ostriches' pen,

I dropped my when the bear startled me,

and I left my with the chimpanzee

when our class took a trip to the zoo.

"My goodness, how did this happen to you

in the short time we've been at the zoo?"

"First, I left my coat with the chimpanzee,

and I dropped my lunch when
the bear startled me.

"Then I tore my pants on the ostriches' pen,

and a button popped off by the lions' den.

"Then my hat blew away
near Billy Goat Mountain,

and my shirt got wet at the water fountain.

"Then my shoes got muddy when I fed a duck,

and my dime rolled under the ice cream truck."

"Oh, dear! I'll bet
you'll be happy
when this day ends."